Text: adaptation by Marilyn Pleau-Murissi and Sarah Margaret Johanson of the animated series
CAILLOU, produced by DHX Media Inc.
All rights reserved.
Illustrations: Eric Sevigny based on the animated series CAILLOU
Coloration: Eric Lehouillier

The PBS KIDS logo is a registered mark of PBS and is used with permission.

Chouette Publishing would like to thank the Government of Canada and SODEC
for their financial support.

Bibliothèque et Archives nationales du Québec and Library and Archives
Canada cataloguing in publication

Main entry under title:
Caillou preschool fun: 2 stories included

Originally published as 2 separate volumes: 2009 and 2012.
Contents: [1]. My first play / Marilyn Pleau-Murissi – [2]. Caillou show and
tell / Sarah Margaret Johanson.

ISBN 978-2-89718-484-1 (hardcover)

1. Schools - Juvenile literature. I. Sévigny, Éric. II. Pleau-Murissi, Marilyn. My
first play. III. Johanson, Sarah Margaret, 1968-   . Caillou show and tell. III.

LB1556.C34 2017   j371   C2017-941922-6

Printed in China
10 9 8 7 6 5 4 3 2 1 CHO2016 SEP2017

Caillou®
Preschool Fun

chouette   dhx media®

Caillou

My First Play

Adaptation of the animated series: Marilyn Pleau-Murissi
Illustrations taken from the animated series and adapted by Eric Sévigny

 chouette dhx media®

Caillou was at day care playing dinosaurs with his friends, Clementine and Leo. Their teacher, Anne, came over to them. "Hello, dinosaurs. Do you remember what we are doing today?"
Caillou, Clementine and Leo looked at each other.

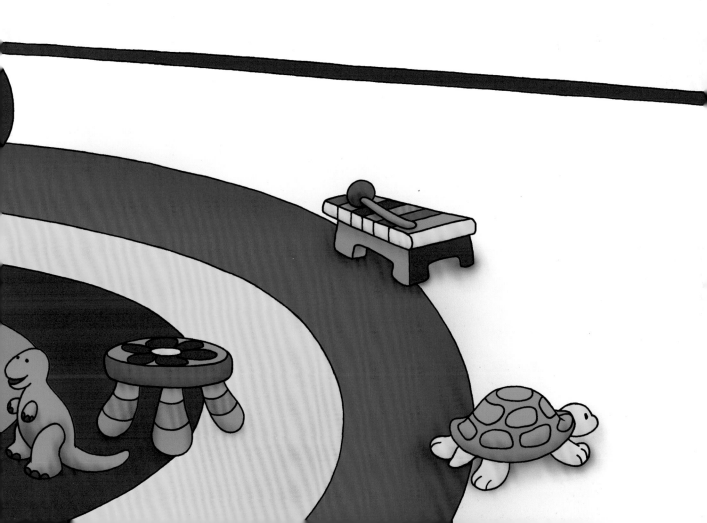

Then Caillou remembered.
"The play, the play!"
he exclaimed.
"That's right!" Anne said.
"YAY!" The children shouted.
"Okay, then let's get started."

There were so many costumes inside the trunk! Caillou and his friends wanted to try them all on. Caillou pulled out a huge red hat and said, "Look, I'm a pirate." Leo found a clown's nose and Clementine put on a witch's hat.

"Remember for this play, we need specific costumes," Anne said. She reached into the trunk and pulled out a sun costume.

"Caillou, you chose the sun, Clementine, you're the flower; and Leo you were going to be a rain cloud."

Anne helped the children dress and said,
"Now, we need a story."
"I'm a beautiful flower," Clementine said.
"Can you make the flower hot and thirsty,
Mr. Sun?" Anne asked Caillou.
Caillou stretched out his arms and Clementine
pretended to be very very thirsty.

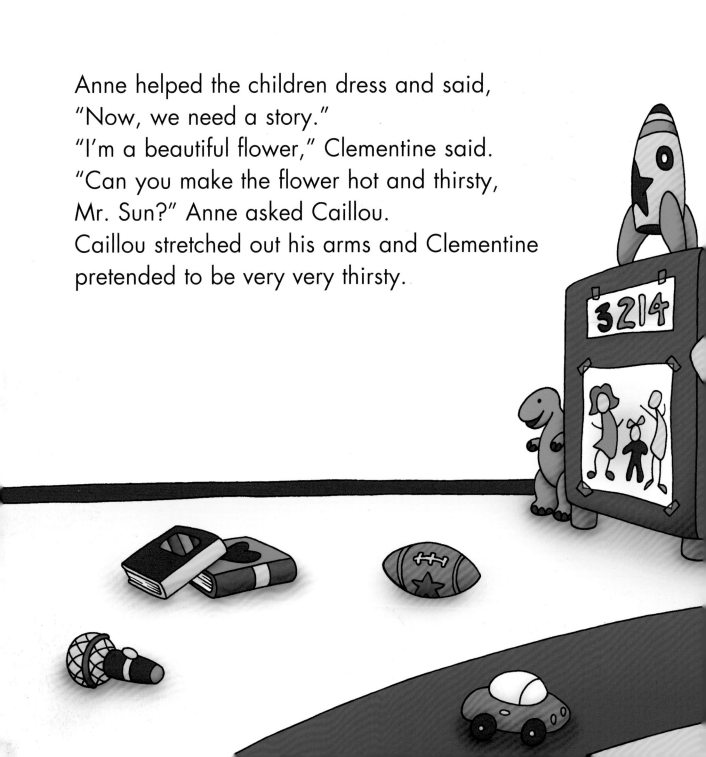

Caillou, Clementine, and Leo laughed and played around. "Okay. Okay," Anne said. "But we need to practice properly. We want to be ready for when your parents arrive. Leo, we need the cloud now." Leo stepped forward and the children practiced all morning.

The parents arrived and were sitting in front of the stage. Behind the curtain, there was a lot of pushing going on.

"It's time... Shh... They're here... Ouch... Stop!"
You could hear Caillou, Leo, and Clementine talking.

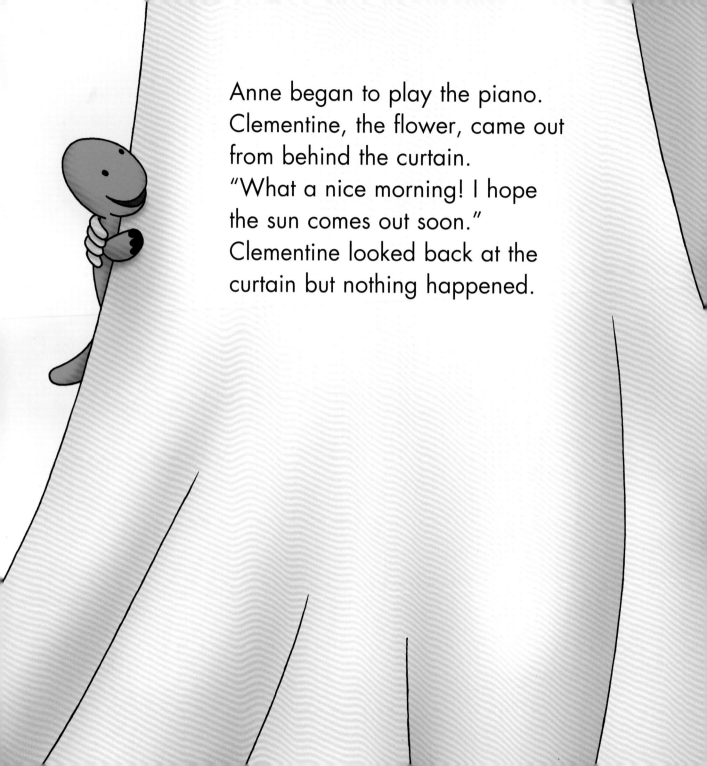

Anne began to play the piano.
Clementine, the flower, came out
from behind the curtain.
"What a nice morning! I hope
the sun comes out soon."
Clementine looked back at the
curtain but nothing happened.

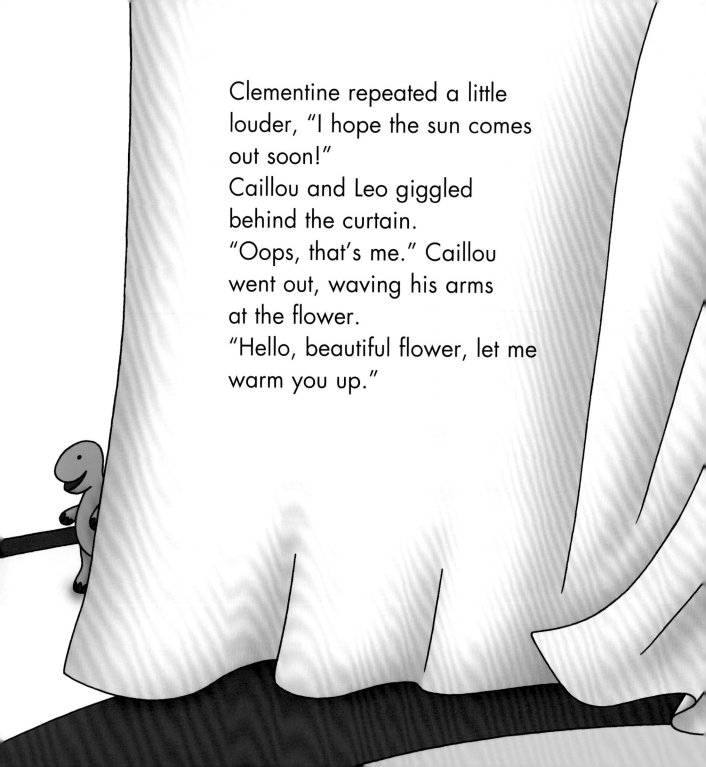

Clementine repeated a little louder, "I hope the sun comes out soon!"
Caillou and Leo giggled behind the curtain.
"Oops, that's me." Caillou went out, waving his arms at the flower.
"Hello, beautiful flower, let me warm you up."

"Oh, the sun is making me so thirsty," Clementine sighed.

Then it was Leo's turn. The rain cloud appeared from behind the curtain and sprinkled water on the flower.

"Thank you, Mr. Cloud," said the flower.

All the parents clapped
their hands and
applauded the children.
Caillou's heart
filled with pleasure.
Clementine and Leo
were happy too.
The sun, the flower,
and the rain cloud then
joined hands and took
a bow.

Caillou

Show And Tell

Adaptation of the animated series: Sarah Margaret Johanson
Illustrations taken from the animated series and adapted by Eric Sévigny

chouette dhx media®

Everyone cleaned up after a fun-filled day of crafts.
"Remember children, tomorrow's show and tell."
"Miss Martin, what's show and tell?" Caillou asked.
"It means that you bring something from home
to show the class, and then you tell us why you
think it's special," Miss Martin explained.

The children were very excited.
"Can I bring something I play with?" Clementine asked.
"Yes, anything you want," Miss Martin replied.
"I know what I'm going to bring. It's a surprise," Leo said.
"Mine's a surprise, too," Clementine said.

Caillou wished he knew what Leo and Clementine were bringing. He wanted to bring a surprise, too.
"Rexy!" Rosie said, playing with the dinosaur.
"I want something that'll be a surprise," Caillou said.
"Surprise, surprise, Caillou!" Rosie sang.

"What are you up to?" Mommy asked.
"I'm trying to find a special surprise for show and tell tomorrow," Caillou said.
"Why don't you choose three things, and you can practice your show and tell on us after supper. Maybe that will help you decide," Mommy said.
Caillou thought that was a very good idea.

After dinner Caillou had a practice show and tell.
"This is Rexy! He's a dinosaur, and he has big teeth, but he isn't mean. He's my favorite toy!" Caillou explained.
"The next surprise is my kite! I took my kite to the park and flew it really high!" Caillou said.
"Rosie fly a kite!" Rosie said, running around the room with the kite.

"And for my last surprise, this is my fire truck! I like it because the ladder goes up and the lights flash," Caillou explained. "So, which one did you like best?"
"They were all special, especially Rexy," Daddy said.
"But Rexy won't be a surprise for Leo," Caillou said.
"And Clementine has already seen my kite."

The next morning, Caillou still did not know which toy would make the best surprise.
"Caillou sad?" Rosie said.
"Miss Martin said we could bring anything we want, but I don't know what to bring," Caillou said.

"SURPRISE!" Rosie cried out to Caillou.
"Daddy, Daddy," Caillou said excitedly.
"What?" Daddy asked, curiously.
"I know what to bring. I need your help,"
Caillou said, and whispered his idea into
Daddy's ear.

The children showed their surprises to their classmates.
"And my grandfather used this compass whenever
he went camping so he wouldn't get lost," Leo explained
as he finished his presentation.
"Miss Martin! My lucky cricket isn't in its cage!"
Clementine panicked. "Everyone look around!"
"I got it!" Leo said.
"Thanks, Leo," Clementine said.
Now she could tell the others about her lucky cricket.

Next it was Caillou's turn to tell his friends about what he had brought for show and tell.
"Are you ready, Caillou?" Daddy was at the door pulling a wagon with a big box covered by a blanket.
"My show and tell is bigger than everyone else's," Caillou said and lifted the blanket.

"SURPRISE!" Rosie exclaimed, jumping out of the box. "I was going to bring one of my favorite toys, but my sister Rosie is even more fun to play with than my toys," Caillou told everyone.